AF251866

Praise for William Shunn's Inclination

"Outstanding . . . [*Inclination*] is told from the point of view of Jude Plane, a young man working on a space station. Jude lives with his father in an enclave of people who follow a traditional religion, a sort of amalgamation of Christianity with respect for the Six Simple Machines. . . . It's a fascinating future, and Jude's personal story is involving."

—Rich Horton, *Locus*

"An intelligent, well-crafted piece. . . . Shunn's elaborate details about the religious rules and philosophies of this group form thought-provoking parallels with some of today's fundamentalist religious groups. It would not surprise me if this tale eventually finds a place in someone's year's best science fiction anthology."

—Jeff Cates, *Tangent*

"A well-considered examination of a basic SF concern: the clash of differing technological levels, and how this (especially now) can cause the lower-tech culture to retreat into fundamentalism. . . . Shunn gets a lot of good satirical digs in, and a contemporary dilemma is penetratingly illuminated."

—Nick Gevers, *Locus*

Shortlisted for
The Hugo Award · The Nebula Award
The Theodore Sturgeon Memorial Award

Inclination

ALSO BY WILLIAM SHUNN

The Accidental Terrorist: Confessions of a Reluctant Missionary
An Alternate History of the 21ˢᵗ Century: Stories
Cast a Cold Eye (with Derryl Murphy)
Our Dependence on Foreign Keys
After the Earthquake a Fire

William Shunn

Inclination

• A Netherview Station Novella •

SINISTER REGARD

New York

2023

Copyright © 2006 by William Shunn
All rights reserved
Published in the United States of America

ISBN 978-1-941-92868-4

Originally published in *Asimov's Science Ficion Magazine*, April/May 2006
First Sinister Regard trade edition: October 2023

www.sinisterregard.com
www.shunn.net

v1.0

Here's looking at you, kid

Inclination

THE MANUAL TELLS US THAT IN THE BEGINNING the Builder decreed six fundamental Machines. These are his six aspects, and all we do we must do with the Six. We need no other machines.

I believe this with all my heart. I do. And yet sometimes I seem to intuit the existence of a seventh Machine, hovering like a blasphemous ghost just beyond apprehension.

There is something wrong with me, and I don't know what it is.

Late for my curfew and trembling, I grasp the doorknob that is not a doorknob.

This is the Machinist Quarter—only a tiny sliver of Netherview Station's Ring B, though I'm one of the few boys I know who has ever been outside it. Fo-grav stays off in the Quarter; our only simulation of gravity is the 0.25 g of natural centripetal acceleration born of the station's rotation and our two-kilometer distance from the hub. We joke that this is why it's called the Quarter. It sure isn't called that after the ratio of its volume to the station's.

The cabin I share with my father Thomas lies in the Inclined Plane branch, third transverse, twelfth hatch on the left. Standing at the hatch, I straighten my billed cap and smooth my coverall—each emblazoned with a right triangle stitched in dove-gray thread, representing our ward—and gently turn the knob. Recessed lights at deck level cast my diffuse shadow up the bulkheads to either side of me. The knob operates as if it were mounted on a genuine mechanical axle, though of course it isn't. A dumb mechanical doorknob wouldn't unlock to my touch alone, or Thomas's. I hate the doorknob. I hate the deceitfulness of it, the way its homogeneous smart matter mimics the virtuous and differentiated and pure. I hate what it conceals. I hate it for not keeping me out.

With a silent prayer to the Builder, I push the hatch open. It swings inward on soundless, lying hinges. I tread lightly inside, in case Thomas is sleeping, the non-slippers on my feet helping me keep my steps short and low. But as I round the door I see Thomas sitting up on his bunk in his short gray underall, watching me enter. The door closes itself behind me, which no door should do unbidden. The cabin is narrow and unadorned but for a diagram of the Six Fundamental Machines affixed to the rear bulkhead, and a small wooden chest bolted to the deck beneath it. The air reeks of a coppery sourness that matches Thomas's narrowed glare. The cabin is so tiny I could reach out and stroke his curly, graying hair if I wanted, but that's an urge that no longer seizes me often. Anyway, the days when I could reliably charm him out of his anger are long past.

"You're late, son," he says. He's squinting at me now, eyes unfocused, the way he does sometimes. He doesn't even glance at the chronometer on his wrist—a true mechanism, with tiny metal gears and not smart matter inside, a symbol of his status as a merchant trader. "It's past your curfew."

"I'm sorry," I say, turning my back and reaching for the crank that will fold my bunk down from the bulkhead opposite his.

His voice grates out in sharp, tight bursts like the strokes of a rasp on iron: "If you were sorry, you'd have been on time."

My shoulder blades prickle. I say nothing, cranking down the bunk.

"Jude, you're fifteen years old," Thomas says. "Why do you think you still have so many rules? Why?"

I try to shrug, but the effort feels jerky, like the gesture of a marionette. "I was waiting my turn at devotions," I say, clinging to the false crank. "You know—with Nic and the rest. But the Foremen wouldn't—they stayed past their time, and we, well . . ."

Thomas has risen, his voice at the back of my neck, shivering my spine. "I was out looking for you. I spoke to Nicodemus an hour ago. In Plane, not at gymnasium."

My blood runs chill. That's two lies I've told, and he's caught me in one already. Nicodemus is my best friend, or used to be, but lately I've been avoiding him. We were up late working on our motors in the schola a couple of weeks ago. He was helping me get the timing right on mine and his fingers brushed the back of my hand. It was just an accident. We've been friends all our lives, but it was like seeing him for the first time. I wanted to touch his face, though I didn't let myself. The scary thing was, it didn't feel wrong, and that scares me all the more.

Of course I can't explain this to Thomas. Nor can I

explain why more and more I can't force myself to evening devotions on time. The cleansing room where we change and shower is like a chamber of horrors. None of the boys seem bothered by disrobing in front of each other, but it bothers me acutely. Letting them see my body makes me want to tear my skin off.

My bunk is halfway lowered. I want to turn and defend myself against Thomas's implicit accusation but a bolus of confusion clogs my throat. Words swarm like dust in my brain, eluding my grasp. Why do I have to explain any of this to him? Why doesn't he just know? And why is it his business?

"Great Builder, Jude," Thomas says at my back, "if you have to lie to me, how can I trust you at a job?"

My shoulders stiffen, my head half turns.

"That's right, I've lined up a job for you. Do you understand, son? At the hub."

A sick despair flares in my gut. Outside the Quarter? Could things get any worse?

"I need you up early, and fresh, but you're out doing Builder knows what when you should be in bed. Did I raise you to be this way, Jude? Did I?"

Tiny flecks of spittle flense the back of my neck. I was at my devotions, I really was, I want to say, but the words won't come.

"Answer me when I speak!" Thomas says, seizing my arm and spinning me around. My cap with its Inclined Plane insignia flies off my head.

The skinny legs tensed for violence, the slow ripple of his round, protruding belly, the sharpening rage on his gray blade of a face—I'm bigger and taller, but I might as well be five again for all that I can stand up to what's coming.

He shakes me. "You will *honor* your father, that your days may be long upon the earth!"

Saline globules tremble at the corners of my eyes, watery jewels sparkling across my sight. The words burst out before I know I'm speaking: "There's no earth here, only metal."

My father's face flushes livid. He spins, hurling me across the cabin—not difficult, since my weight is just twenty kilos. I sprawl across my father's bunk, all gawky limbs and terror.

I roll over and there he is looming above me, fists raised and shaking. It's been months since last he struck me, an improbable lucky streak which now seems about to end. But he lowers his arms and leans over me.

"The Wrecker's in you, boy," he says, shaking a finger. "You pray hard and shake loose his grip. Pray to be made square and true. Tomorrow more than ever, you need the Builder to be with you."

And now he's pulling on his coverall and leaving the cabin to stalk off his anger, the hatch snicking shut behind him like a quiet tap to a finishing nail. Alone, I flow off the bunk to the floor, to my knees, to retrieve my cap and pray.

I'm out of true and I need fixing. Through shuddering tears I pray for the Builder to make me a better son, a stronger laborer, a whole person. I pray for his protection, both physical and spiritual. I pray for reassurance that Thomas doesn't really mean to send me alone among the Sculpted in the morning.

When I finally crawl into my bunk and wrap the blanket around myself, though, it's not the Builder with his Machines I picture watching over me in the dark. It's my departed mother Kaiya, angel wings spread above me in a canopy of white.

THE BUILDER HAS IGNORED MY PRAYER, AT LEAST the part about the Sculpted.

We rise and dress early, Thomas and I, and exit our cabin. In one hand Thomas carries a gray cloth sack big enough to hold a loaf of bread.

Only the most devoted practitioners are awake at this hour, en route to gymnasium. Rather than follow them, Thomas leads me to the end of the next branch over, to where Saul, foreman of Inclined Plane, lives. The only mark that sets this hatch apart from every other in the row is the small carpenter's square etched at its very center.

Foreman Saul appears in the hatchway, bleary-eyed, at Thomas's knock. "Selah, Jude," he says in greeting, favoring me with a look both compassionate and foreboding. "Brother Thomas, let me speak to you alone a moment. We'll only be a bit, Jude."

Thomas follows Saul inside without a glance at me. I stand in the corridor and mentally rehearse the Builder's Code. I'm still in Lever, less than halfway through the Hexalogue, when the hatch opens again. Saul gestures me in.

The cabin is a little smaller than the one Thomas and I share, and consequently more crowded than ours ever gets. Thomas sits at one end of the only bunk, cloth sack in his lap. He pats the space beside him, and I sit. Saul picks up a thermos from the foldout stovetop that juts from the rear bulkhead and sips carefully at the spout. The air smells faintly of powdered coffee and machine oil.

"Jude," Saul says, "your father let me know late last night that he's secured you a position on a stevedore crew at the docks. Unfortunately, as you're required there promptly this morning and you can now be fined for tardiness, there's no time to go through the usual series of preparatory lessons before you leave the safety of the Quarter."

I don't miss the baleful sideways glance Saul gives Thomas, but Thomas doesn't seem to react to it. He just sits there with the same twist of bored impatience on his lips.

"Oh, I've been out a couple of times before," I say, if only to cut the palpable tension, which is settling into my neck. "I mean, when I was younger."

"Yes." Saul sighs, blinking his pouchy eyes a few times. He is older than my father, taller and softer, but no sadder. I've been tempted many times to bring my cares and questions to him, but something has always held me back. "You're a bright young man, Jude, and I know you've walked among the Sculpted before, so at least the sights won't be new to you. But accompanying your father once or twice on his rounds is hardly the same as working alongside them, alone, for a full shift every day. If there's no time for the proper instruction first, at the very least a blessing is in order."

"Okay," I say, a little of the weight lifting from my shoulders. Even if the Builder isn't listening to me, surely he'll listen to the foreman, as pious a man as I know. But at the same time I'm beginning to feel in my gut just how much spiritual danger I'll be courting. Why is Thomas doing this to me?

"If you'll sit here?" Saul says. He is setting up a metal folding chair in the middle of the cabin, which means it nearly bumps Thomas's knees. I scoot over into the chair, doffing my cap and clutching it in my lap, as Saul removes a ceremonial oilcan from a niche in the bulkhead. Thomas joins Saul behind me. The oilcan *ka-chunks*, the tip of its spout tickling the hair at the crown of my head as it deposits a tiny bead of machine oil. Saul gently taps the droplet down onto my scalp, and he and Thomas lay their hands upon my head.

Other kids get to have their mothers in the cabin with them during blessings like this. I close my eyes and try to imagine Kaiya here, watching from the corner near the hatch. And she could be, right? Surely that's not a vain hope.

"Great Builder," Saul says, "in the name of the Wheel,

the Wedge, the Lever, the Plane, the Pulley, and the Screw, we bring before you your true and faithful servant Jude, who ventures forth this day to labor amongst the Sculpted for his daily bread. Be with him, Builder, that he might have health in his navel, marrow in his bones, and strength in his sinews—strength that he might work and not be weary, but moreso that the Wrecker with his subtle wiles may find no purchase in his heart, mind, or flesh. We know the Wrecker's cunning is great, Builder, and that he can make what's wrong seem right. But your power and love are infinite, and so we commend this young man to your oversight with all faith in your goodness and wisdom. May we ever draw nearer to thee, Great Builder, as the Inclined Plane rises ever to heaven. Amen."

"Amen," I say. The hands, which have grown progressively heavier during the blessing, lift from my head. I stand, rolling my head to soothe my neck.

Saul folds the chair and sets it aside—a deft, practiced move in the cramped space—then reaches out to clasp my forearm in the Scaffold Grip. His hand is warm and dry. "What's today, Thursday? Let's meet Sundays after temple, Jude, to make some headway on those lessons. Better late than never."

"When his schedule allows," Thomas says, conspicuously checking his chronometer. "They call this Oneday outside. Weeks aren't reckoned the same."

"Of course. Then any day you can, Jude." Saul squeezes and releases my forearm. "And remember that the Builder blesses you not just for obedience to his commandments, but for obedience to your parents as well."

"Jude," Thomas says. He picks the sack up from the bunk and inclines his head toward the hatch.

"Selah, Foreman," I say and follow my father out into the corridor. I look back to see, in the moment before the hatch closes behind us, Foreman Saul standing like a forlorn beast in the center of a cage.

Or is that perception just a way to make myself feel better about the sentence to which I've been condemned?

Thomas leads me at a brisk pace out to the main corridor, skipping lightly along the deck. "Don't let him get to you, Jude," he says over his shoulder. "Saul, Bartholomew, none of the Foremen understand our economic realities."

I'm not sure whether he means our family's or the whole Quarter's. I don't ask for clarification, not just because I don't like encouraging him to disparage the Foremen but because we've turned into the main corridor and a few more people, from all different wards, are out and about now. The soft gray of their coveralls and visored caps against the brighter gray of the bulkheads make the Quarter look almost like a scene from an ancient monochrome photograph.

We pass the gymnasium entrance, then the intersections with Wedge Branch and Wheel and Axle. We're alone now, and the Primum Mobile Gate looms ahead, painted with various strident warnings and danger symbols.

"You'll have to find your own way back this evening, so pay close attention," Thomas says, pulling the lever that opens the Gate. The massive hatch grinds aside, admitting a bedlam of voices and light and sound. "Now be ready for the weight. And whatever you do, don't gawk."

My heart races. I follow Thomas through the Gate and an extra forty kilos drops onto my bones. Thanks to my faithful attention to devotions I don't fall, but I stagger and I'm sweating in the moist air before we've gone far. The public corridors are as crowded and noisy now as they are around the clock, alive with the babel of a thousand languages, and the bulkheads are lost in the riot of greenery that thrives on every available surface. I feel conspicuous in my Machinist garb. People—monsters—fall silent and stare as we pass, and with all their unsettling modifications it's hard not to stare back. I can't imagine navigating this profane world without Thomas.

We ride a slidewalk spinward, then crowd into a hubward elevator that at least contains no obvious plant life. But for every normal person, I see one with skin the wrong color or texture, limbs numbering too many or too few, a body with mysterious prosthetics or protuberances, or a head misshapen and gross. A pebbled gray creature that might once have been human brushes against me in the elevator. Dizzy, I press closer to Thomas, the sweat trickling into my eyes. I'm not sure whether his hand on my shoulder is meant to reassure me or restrain me.

At hub level, the bulkheads are again clean and metallic, as they should be. Thomas leads me through a short but bewildering maze of hatches and gangways. With fewer people around now, I breathe more easily. Thomas knocks at an open hatch. I peek inside. It's an office about a meter and a half in radius, and every surface, 720 spherical degrees around, is jammed with monitors, control panels, and handholds. The thickset woman seated at the center has a second pair of arms where her legs should be.

"I don't give a spout for your schedule," she tells someone unseen. "My stevies can do the job fast, but not that fast. All right, fine. You do that."

She looks at Thomas, and I see she has silver semispheres implanted over her eyes. Three quick swings from handhold to handhold bring her to the door. Fograv is still about 0.75. She's *strong*.

"This the kid?" she asks.

"That's him," Thomas says.

She turns those reflective bugeyes on me, twitching her head up and down, and it's like I'm being X-rayed. What she sees, I can't imagine. "Any mods? No, of course not. You goddamn Wheelies, what am I talking about? All right, he doesn't look too bad. Let's get him suited up and see how he does. What's your name, kid?"

My mouth is so dry my tongue crackles. "Jude."

"Well, now you're Stevie. For stevedore."

She barks a laugh like a chugging motor, clinging to holds around the hatch with three hands. Thomas laughs too. His eyes crinkle and his lips peel back, and it's like seeing ten years drop away from him. He never laughs around me.

In that moment I feel inexpressibly sad. And I hate him.

The woman swings out through the hatch and drops to the deck between Thomas and me. "Follow me," she says, loping down the gangway on all fours.

Thomas shoves the cloth sack into my hands. "Your lunch," he says.

I clutch the sack like a lifeline. It's three times as heavy as it should be, and its heft brings a desperate lump to my throat. On a usual morning, it's I who makes lunch for Thomas, but I didn't even think about it today. I'm realizing that the usual mornings are behind me.

"Now you work hard and do what Renny tells you," Thomas says. "I can't stress enough how important this money is."

"Okay." I turn to trudge after the woman.

"And remember who you are," Thomas stage-whispers fiercely. "Your body belongs to the Builder, not to them."

"Selah," I say.

Thomas sighs. "Selah, son. Now go."

Renny, fidgeting impatiently, has stopped at a juncture up ahead. I follow, the grief of abandonment thick in my throat.

THE SIX ARE MORE THAN JUST MACHINES. HIGH
Foreman Titus—our founder, who 120 years ago spoke
with the Builder face to face—teaches us that they rep-
resent the Builder's various aspects, and thus the ways
in which we must approach him. The Six also name our
wards, the clans or tribes of our faith. Though my father
and I belong to Inclined Plane Ward, we owe each equal
adoration, and it's the Wedge that concerns me now.

The Manual teaches that the purpose of the Wedge is
to both divide asunder and hold in place. From this we
learn to divide ourselves from the evils of the world, as
the maul divides the log, keeping always to the side of
the Builder. Yet we also learn to bridge the gap between,
as the keystone—a truncated wedge—holds the arch in
place. The lesson for us is to serve the world, and serve
as examples, without becoming corrupted by it.

As a people, we excel at dividing ourselves from the

world. We don't do so well at bridging—except perhaps for my father. But between him and me there's surely a great Wedge, and it's never clear to me which of us is on which side of it.

THOMAS DIDN'T EXPLAIN TO ME EXACTLY WHAT A stevedore is. Turns out it's someone who loads and unloads cargo. Starships from hundreds of light-years around dock at Netherview Station's hub, then, depending on size and mass, slide into one of three concentric levels of berths. Many of the ships are laded automatically by robot or waldo; the ones that can't afford the special treatment (or can afford to waive it) get us.

Renny explains this to me, more colorfully, as I follow her to the locker room. She leaves me alone there to change into my docksuit, a close-fitting layer of red polymer that covers me from the neck down. I try not to think about how much smart matter I must be wearing. I leave my coverall and cap behind like a shed snakeskin in my thumbprint-activated locker. The heaviness I feel has nothing to do with gravity, though physically I'm breathing hard already from the exertion since leaving the Quarter. Carrying my lunch sack, I rejoin my new boss outside the locker room.

Before leading me to the berth where the crew awaits us, Renny rears up on her hind arms and affixes a round green badge to my chest. "Regs," she says. "Since you've got no built-in monitors, this'll let us keep tabs on you."

The crew is twelve, male and female both, and I make thirteen. They're lounging in a small break room off Berth C-46. Renny clambers to the top of a table and waves for quiet. "This is our new trainee," she says. "His name is Jude Plane. Corgie, he's your man this shift."

A groan from a preternaturally thin fellow sprawled out on a couch prompts laughter from the others and a sinking feeling inside me. I'm sweating, much to my embarrassment.

"Okay, you shits, okay. The *Needlethreader*'s in dock now. Let's go."

The crew don helmets and begin to spill out a hatch opposite the one Renny brought me through. They disperse in all directions—left, right, up, down—grabbing implements from a rack outside as they go. They're all human in shape, mostly normal as far as I can see. They don't look much older than I am, but you never can tell with the Sculpted. One has bright blue skin above the collar of his suit, an eye-straining contrast with the red polymer. He winks at me as he drops out the hatch. My stomach clenches.

Renny hops down from the table and grabs Corgie by the leg before he can say a word to me. "Pay close attention to the kid," Renny says. "He's barefoot. He'll need a fishbowl on top of everything else."

"You're joking," Corgie says. "I don't think I've ever seen a fishbowl."

"There's one in the rack today along with everything else."

My trainer heaves an aggrieved sigh. "All right, Juke," he says to me. "Follow me and stick close."

"Jude," I say.

"Right. Juke."

Renny reaches for my lunch sack, which I still clutch uncertainly. She stashes it for me as I trail out the hatch after Corgie.

And suddenly I'm not just lighter. I'm weightless, and drifting.

Fo-grav isn't turned off in the berth; it's on but dialed down to null, damping even the small inertial effects of rotational velocity and centrifugal force. Corgie gives me a brief lesson in how to maneuver in null-g with a dock-wand, a thin, meter-long rod of smart matter that ejects a stream of inert particles from one end or the other on command. Basically you point it, squeeze, and drift off in the opposite direction. It takes me a while to get the hang of it, largely because I'm loath to touch it, but soon enough I'm helping Corgie and the rest carry out the dockwand's other function, herding big gray crates of who knows what out of the cargo hold in the belly of the starship and through the air to the elevators that will take them wherever they need to go next—sometimes another level of the station, sometimes the hold of an-other ship in another berth.

I do it all wearing a helmet with a transparent visor that curves down over my face. The helmet draws words and diagrams in the air, overlaying what I see, giving me data like what time of day it is and where the next crate needs to go. By turning my head and focusing somewhere, I can get information about whatever I'm looking at. Sweeping my gaze along the streamlined, almost organic curve of the huge ship, for example, I can access its flight schedules, crew data, cargo manifests, manufacturer's specifications, and even schematic diagrams that show me more of what it looks like than I can possibly see by just flitting around in the space between its black belly and the berth's bulkhead. I can zoom in on the other crews working the hatches fore and aft of ours, and I can even find out more about my own crewmates, though I don't feel right about prying. But it *is* a good way to learn everyone's name, which I manage before the start of our first break.

Is this the world my crewmates walk through every waking moment of every day, with intimate information about everything they see just an eyeblink away? We may inhabit the same great wheel in space, but these strangers live in a truly alien world, one I don't like visiting. Builder knows making motors isn't my favorite activity, good as I am at it; still, I'd rather be in my applied mechanics class with Nic and Mal than here. I'd even rather be home with Thomas—anywhere but stranded amongst the ignorantly blasphemous, wielding tools that are an offense in the sight of the Builder, being slowly poisoned by the worldview of the Sculpted.

What is Thomas trying to do to me?

Our shift is the longest day of my life. The ghostly ticking clock in the corner of my vision doesn't help.

AT SHIFT'S END WE DEPOSIT OUR DOCKWANDS, now stubby and depleted, in the rack outside the break room and file off to the showers. I'm happy to drop off my fishbowl as well, though the experience of walking in gravity without a data overlay seems somehow dream-like and crippling as I readjust to moving about with-out it—almost as crippling as walking in high-g alone. It surprises me how exhausted I am. I must have used and abused every muscle in my body.

As we reach the locker room, I'm startled that our sin-gle-file queue remains intact. The women enter through the same hatch as the men. Bringing up the rear, I tell myself there must surely be a dividing bulkhead or at the very least a screen inside, but of course I was here this morning and know there's no such thing. I try to keep my eyes averted, but just to reach my locker I must step around a woman named Soon, who already has her suit pushed down to her hips.

The room is too small, and everyone jostles everyone else on the way to the ultrasonic showers. I stand with my burning face to my open locker, wondering if I can get away with standing here and not changing until the room is empty. Soon's bare torso blazes like a beacon in my mind. A part of me is fascinated and wants to look at it again; another part is horrified at the thought, and at the distant, epochal memories of my mother that stir, memories so ancient they seem apocryphal.

Renny, galumphing through the locker room, slaps the back of my thigh and says, "Next shift's gotta get in, kid. Hurry it up."

Somehow I strip off the suit, deposit it in the recycler, and manage the walk to the showers. My skin crawls as I crowd into the white ceramic chamber with the others, though part of this, I'm sure, is the feel of the ultrasonics vibrating sweat and grime loose from my body. Still, I can't look higher than anyone's ankles. It's not just the naked flesh that distresses me. I'm out of my coverall in front of heathen, and that's a grave offense in the sight of the Builder. My hands hover in front of my crotch.

My hip brushes the thin blue man's; I nearly jump out of my skin, and I mumble an apology. "Don't worry about it," he says with a kind smile. "We're all friends here."

"Yeah," Corgie says. "Just help yourself to a handful of whatever's closest."

"Or a thimbleful," says an apparent neuter named Ice IX, pointing at Corgie's flaccid penis.

"Careful. You don't want to wake the monster."

Mijk, a muscular man with a series of knobby lumps down his back, says, "I do. Someone ran all the lotion out of my dispenser."

"And apparently he wants it back," Soon says with a giggle.

Corgie wipes his mouth. "Come and get it," he says, and his penis flares to enormous size, all ridged and quivering. It *is* a monster.

I turn away, blushing. But something strange has begun to happen. I don't feel comfortable exactly, but I do feel somewhat invisible, with less of the compulsion to run and hide than comes in the cleansing room at gymnasium. I'm able to let my eyes roam some, taking in the female bodies as well as the male, plus two or three I find less determinate and the entirely genderless Ice IX. In the Quarter, contact between boys and girls is strictly regulated and chaperoned, even during courtship; a situation like this is as unthinkable as a motor assembling itself from raw ore. I have more answers now than I know what to do with to what minutes ago was only a compelling mystery.

I almost don't want the shower to end, but when the thought takes form I realize the Wrecker is already getting his claws into me. How much easier a time of it he has here than inside the Quarter! Despair washes over me. How will I ever survive this?

Clean, but with a film of shame clinging to my exposed skin, I trail the group back to the lockers. I've pulled on my underall and my coverall and am about to put my cap on when a tall, trouserless man named Twenty plucks it deftly out of my hands.

"What's this for, some kind of uniform?" he asks, turning the cap this way and that. "You got *another* job?"

My muscles seem to seize up, and the bottom falls out of my soul. So much for invisibility. Renny is gone; I don't know where to turn for help. Heat and mortification radiate from the top of my uncovered head as Twenty's Sculpted hands defile my cap.

"No, you ramscoop," Corgie says, taking the cap, "he's a Wheelie. Don't you know anything?"

And now he's passing it to someone else, who's asking why there's a triangle on it if I'm a Wheelie, and now it goes to someone else, and now it's flying through the air past my face, and now again the other way. I reach for the cap, but it's snatched by the knobby-spined Mijk.

"Wheelie, huh?" he says. "Those are like Christers, right? How come you're named after a traitor, Wheelie?"

"*Judas* betrayed the Builder," I say quietly. I want to sound dangerous, but even I can hear the quaver in my voice. "Jude was a different apostle."

"Jude, Judas, Peter, penis—whatever. Think this'd fit me?"

Mijk's about to slip the cap onto his head, and I'm about to shout something, maybe do something I'll regret, when a half-dressed woman named Beneficent Sunrise takes it from him.

"Mijk, it doesn't stretch. It's not smart enough to fit your thick skull."

"Then what good is it?"

Beneficent Sunrise turns the cap over. She studies the inclined plane symbol. "Never seen something made from dumb fabric before. Interesting the way it feels. Almost real."

Her frank curiosity defuses my anger. Or is it the sight of her full, bobbing breasts? They fill me with an emotion I can't quite put a name to. Not desire, not quite, but something as sharp in its poignancy. I wonder what *they* feel like.

The blue man picks my cap cleanly out of her grip. Holding it by the visor only, he puts it in my hand. My fingers clutch it spasmodically.

"Real like your tits, Sunny?" he says to the woman.

"Go deplete your wand," she says in the general laughter, but she's smiling with everyone else.

Weak with humiliation and relief, I cover my head and turn to rummage in my empty locker. Around me, my crewmates casually hide their nakedness.

The blue man is called Haun Friedrich 4, but the fishbowl taught me he prefers to go by Derek Specter. He's in the trial period before a legal name change.

The idea that one may choose one's own name is as strange to me as everything else about the Sculpted. What would I choose if I were to name myself? Paul? Luke? Timothy? None of them work. I can't imagine learning to answer to any name but Jude. That's me. That's who I am.

I'm standing in the gangway outside the locker room, having lingered there until the arriving crew forced me out. People edge past me in both directions. I'm trying to remember which way I came this morning, fighting a growing sense of panic, when Haun—Derek—touches my shoulder with blue fingers.

"Know where you're going?" he asks with an easy grin.

"Er…rimward," I say, feeling the blood heat my cheeks.

"Yes, that would almost certainly be correct." Derek leans against the bulkhead near me, a little too close, arms folded and eyes bright. His skin is the blue of Enoch's fabled seas, and his irises glow like bits of its sky. "Do you need any help getting there?"

I look down at my gray nonslippers. "I guess I do," I say, embarrassed at the prospect of this ostentatiously abnormal creature rescuing me twice in the same ten minutes.

Derek gazes at the opposite bulkhead, cupping his chin. "Wheelieville, I presume," he says. He gives me a sidelong glance, apologetic but not self-conscious. "The Machinist Quarter, I mean."

"Uh, yeah."

His eyes narrow. "Let me just find it on the map."

"What map?" I say. His glance this time is mildly reproving, and I let out an abashed "Oh."

"We just need to get you to Elevator Seven, Eight, or Nine," Derek says after a moment. "That's probably the trickiest part of the route. And I happen to be going the same way, if you don't mind company."

My feet are itching to move. I'd rather he just point me in the right direction and let me go my way, but I'm too tired to argue. I shrug my acquiescence.

As we set off down the narrow way, Derek says over his shoulder, "You were good in there today. Not everyone adjusts to null-gee that quickly. I think even Renny was impressed."

He looks back expectantly, but since I'm not sure what I'm supposed to say to this, I don't answer.

"Corgie gave you some shit, I know," Derek says, "but you should have seen him back when he started. Talk about an ostrich. Was this your first time with an overlay?"

"Yes."

"I remember when I was first getting used to it. It was strange to turn it off and not see labels everywhere I looked. You must be going through the same thing. You probably haven't ever used Geoff before either." At my blank look, he grins. "Yeah, we'll have to teach you how to use Geoff. Then next time you need to get somewhere you won't have to put up with me running off at the mouth."

"What's Geoff?" I ask.

"Info daemon on the public net. You've really been sheltered, haven't you? Geoff's mostly for travelers and transients—anyone offline, really, so you can use him too. He'll answer any question you have, if he has the answer and you're older than ten. And as long as it's not private or classified."

Derek keeps looking back at me with an expression like he's trying to tell me something significant and I'm just not getting it. I feel dumb, and my skin's been crawling ever since the word "daemon" anyway. "I—thanks, but that doesn't sound like something I ought to be messing with."

He gives me one more look, then shrugs. "Suit yourself," he says. "But you do have a right to whatever information you want. You only have to ask."

We take the next couple of turns in silence, me adrift

in an uneasiness I can't quite put my finger on.

"So what's a nice Machinist like you doing in a job like this anyway?" Derek asks at last. "I thought you were supposed to stick to your own turf, not venture out amongst the unwashed."

The corridors are wider now, the crowds thickening, and Derek, walking beside me, speaks too loudly for my comfort. "Commerce with the Sculpted isn't forbidden," I say a little defensively, keeping my voice low. "It's just... discouraged, I guess. It's—there's a lot of danger, spiritually."

"I always wanted to be a spiritual hazard," Derek says. "You probably shouldn't even be talking to me, should you?"

"Um . . ." I'm looking around, anywhere but at him. There are unholy forms and faces and sounds and smells everywhere. "Not really, not like this."

"So why are you? I mean, in the larger sense. Why are you here at all? Why do you have this job?"

I sigh. "I didn't exactly have a choice," I say, cursing my inability to hold my tongue. "Thomas, my father, he's our ward trader, which means he goes out and sells whatever we build or manufacture. That's so the ward can meet its obligation to the Guild."

"Which is saving up to get off Netherview Station and continue its fabled trek to Enoch. I've read about it."

I look at him, nonplussed. We know so little about the Sculpted, I somehow can't get over the fact they know anything about us. "But business isn't so good," I continue. "As trader, my father has to pay the rest of the ward first, before he takes his share, but lately there's not much left over. In fact, I think there may not be anything left over. He's been trying for months to get me a job outside the Quarter, and believe me, that means things are grim."

"Of course they are," Derek says. "Who wants primitive toys made from primitive materials?"

"They're not toys!" I say, turning on him, thinking of the motor I've been building for some weeks now. "It's serious work! It's sacred!"

"Hey, hey, I'm sorry." We're now at the elevator bay, waiting, and Derek puts his hands up as if to ward off my anger. I see for the first time that his palms and the pads of his fingers are a rich green, fading into blue at the edges. "I didn't mean it like that. But you have to realize that's how most people see what you do. If it has no practical use, it must be a toy."

"It does have a practical use," I say. "You people are just too stiffnecked to humble yourselves and admit it."

Derek nods. "Or you might say we've put away childish things."

This reference to the Manual startles me. The elevator opens as I'm groping for a suitable reply, and we crowd in with several other commuters, including a woman who has tentacles where her fingers should be. Derek spends the ride staring straight ahead with the barest of smiles on his lips.

I'm still smarting when the elevator opens on Six. I'm about to say that I think I can find my way from here, but Derek steps out with me into the thick, damp air and dank vegetation.

"I've been meaning to ask," he says, "what *is* the significance of the triangle on your clothing? It's an inclined plane, right?"

"Um, right," I say. "That's the ward I belong to."

"You're lucky you're not in Screw," he says. "You'd never hear the end of it at work."

"So, er," I say, stumbling a little as we step onto the counterspinward slidewalk, "I guess you understand the Inclined Plane is one of the Six Fundamental Machines."

"I've heard that rumor somewhere," Derek says.

"Well, they're also symbols. This one represents the obliqueness of our approach to the Master Builder. No matter—"

"You mean God, right?"

"You might call him that," I say.

"I might. And again, I might not."

He has a way of continually derailing me and looking pleased about it that I find entirely infuriating. "No matter how shallow the angle," I say, soldiering on, "the Inclined Plane leads us ever upward, and though it may take eons, eventually we'll reach the level of the Builder."

"Sounds suspiciously like the Tower of Babel," Derek says. "And didn't God punish the Babylonians for trying to approach him in just that way?"

"Their approach was more direct, and completely literal," I say, my voice heating up. "We're not talking about a literal approach. Ours is metaphorical. We approach the Builder by understanding and manipulating his six aspects."

"I'd have thought he'd have more respect for the direct approach. You know, just wrap an inclined plane around a big pole and climb to heaven." He waggles his blue eyebrows at me, eyes twinkling. "Maybe what offended him about it was the metaphorical significance of it. Maybe the Babylonians were really saying God could screw himself, and that's why he gave them all a good tongue-lashing."

The delight he derives from such extreme statements takes my breath away. "You can't approach the Builder in anything but a metaphorical way!" I say.

"Then why let yourselves be literally constrained? Why confine yourselves to what you can build from six fairly arbitrary machines?"

"The machines aren't arbitrary! They're the six aspects of the Builder."

"They are arbitrary, and not all of them are even that fundamental. The screw we were just talking about—like I said, it's just an inclined plane wrapped around an axle. The pulley's a special case of the wheel and axle, and the wedge is just another way of looking at an inclined plane."

I wipe fatigue sweat from my forehead. He's hitting uncomfortably close to blasphemous thoughts I've entertained myself, which may explain my vehemence in denouncing them. "Every aspect partakes of the others to some extent," I say, but I sound more shrill than certain.

"Seems to me that if there really is a god, you could find some far more useful metaphors for the way he operates if you'd just reach deeper than your six machines."

He exits the slidewalk and I follow, belatedly realizing we've arrived near the PM Gate. To my relief and chagrin both, I've been so focused on the conversation that I haven't paid much attention to the nightmarish creatures around me, nor to the riotous greenery. But I notice them all now and feel hemmed in.

"We're not meant to reach deeper," I say, hurrying to keep up with Derek's long gait in the swarming crowd.

"Then you'll never achieve godhood, now, will you?" Derek says. He pauses near the unadorned hatchway that leads to the Machinist Quarter. "Well, here you are."

Bathed in sweat, I purse my lips. "Thanks, uh . . . thanks for getting me here."

"The pleasure was all mine." He makes as if to move on, but stops. "I meant to tell you before, I thought you handled those jokers in the locker room about as well as you could have. Just don't let them know they're getting to you and they'll leave you alone soon enough. They're not really mean, just exemplars of what I call the indolent uninformed. Learning new things is such a trivial process they don't even make the effort."

"Like the Israelites and the fiery serpents," I say.

Derek blinks, his eyes losing focus. "Interesting," he says after a moment or two. "Numbers, chapter twenty-one. If the ones who were bitten only gazed upon Moses's brass serpent, they would live. All they had to do was look. You know, there's good sense to be found in that book here and there."

"The miracle is," I say, "even a gentile can look and see it."

Derek laughs long and loud. It makes me feel clever and proud, though why I should care about looking clever to this mockery of a man baffles me. "Touché, Jude," he says. "See you tomorrow at the orifice."

He studies some resource invisible to me, and then he's off, a lean blue figure vanishing into a teeming, grotesque jungle. I'm reminded that he inhabits a world even more strange than this physical one, and that when the two or us look at an object we each see a vastly different thing.

"Selah, Derek," I say under my breath. I pull the lever and pass through the Gate, wondering what he sees when he looks at me.

THE CLEANLINESS, CALM, COOL, AND QUIET OF the Quarter stand in stark contrast to what I've left behind. It's evening by our clocks; we run here on only one shift. The few Machinists out and about look at me strangely as I pass from outside. It should feel good, this homecoming after an eternal shift away, this shedding of weight, this lightness, this cooling of my sweat, but I find myself keyed up and restless before I've even reached the branching to Wheel and Axle. I know Thomas will be waiting for me, wanting to know how the day went, but I can't confine myself at home just yet. Instead I lower my head and trudge to gymnasium.

The machines are manned mostly by Levers, all older than I, but one station opens up before long. I do my best to complete the ritual properly, pitting every muscle group against the pulleys as I rehearse the Builder's Code in my mind, but I'm barely into the first canto before my sore muscles are quaking. What's more, I can't keep my thoughts focused. My mind keeps reaching back to worry images of naked flesh—sometimes colored naturally, sometimes blue or green.

One by one the Levers are finishing up and heading to the cleansing room, some of them whispering and giving me looks as strange as the ones I got outside from the Sculpted. I rush to try to complete the minimal requirements before the place fills up with Inclined Planes, but in vain. I'm not quite done when Nicodemus and another Plane named Amos arrive. I see them from across the room, over the tops of three ranks of machines. I duck my head but too late. Nic spots me and hurries over.

The station next to mine is empty, abandoned just moments before. Nic, his face cautiously friendly, slides into the seat, leaving Amos to fidget awkwardly in the aisle before us. "Selah, Jude," Nic says.

"Selah," I say, mouth dry.

Nic begins some warmup stretches of his arms and back. "You weren't at schola today," he says.

I look straight ahead, pumping away with my arms in bellows mode, but Amos is right there staring at me so I focus on my knees instead. "No," I say.

"Malachi heard you were outside," Nic says.

"Yeah, at the hub," Amos says.

"He said you had a job."

A wary hope fills Nic's voice, but whether it's hope that the rumors or true or simply hope that I'll talk to him, I can't tell. Either way, I can't look at him. I can't look at his golden hair, his glistening shoulders, his wise blue eyes. But I can't not answer.

"That's right," I say gruffly. "I guess you won't see me much in class anymore."

"Is it true about the Sculpted?" Amos says. He's a skinny kid and he practically dances from foot to foot. "They drink blood instead of water?"

"Amos, I see a free machine over there," Nic says with a jerk of his head.

"But—"

"I'm nearly done here," I say.

"Better hurry, Amos."

I can't see Nic's face, but I hear the tone of warning in his voice, and I see the answering expression of querulousness on Amos's face. Amos stalks off, even as I fight down the unwelcome surge of warm emotion in my chest.

I rest for a twelve-count, saying nothing, then embark on another bellows set.

Nic has launched into a set of cherrypickers. "So what's with you, Jude?" he says between reps.

"What do you mean?"

"You've been avoiding me for a couple of weeks now. What did I do?"

I sigh, clinging to the handgrips and letting my upper body sag. "It's not you, Nic."

"Then what is it? Is it about this job?"

What am I supposed to tell him? That I've started to worry I like him too much? I can hardly express the thought even to myself.

"It's not about the stupid job," I say, though I'm aching to tell him about everything I've seen and done today. I cut my set short and stand up, infuriated. "Great Builder, you're so—so—oh, flashcan it!"

I rush to the cleansing room with all the dignity I can muster, which isn't much, aware of all the eyes on me. In the quick glimpse I caught of Nic before I fled, there was hurt and concern. He hadn't yet broken a sweat.

I try to put him out of my head among the straggling Levers in the steam-filled shower. I try to conjure the illusion of camouflage I felt in the showers at the hub, as if I could hide myself amongst my Sculpted crewmates and never be seen. Here I feel anxious and wrong, like I don't belong. But I certainly don't belong there.

Scanting my cleansing, I dress quickly and hurry into the main corridor. The crowds here are about as thick as they ever get but seem downright sparse compared to outside. People stride lightly from their duties back to their branches, men and women, boys and girls, as evening stretches toward the dinner hour. I envy them their apparent lack of care.

"Jude, Jude," hails a gentle voice, and I raise my head. I hadn't realized my neck had bent as if in stronger gravity.

It's Sariah, a Pulley my age who's walking the other way. "Oh, selah," I say.

She takes my sleeve and draws me to the side of the corridor. "Missed you at schola," she says, voice low. Not that we have any of the same classes, but the boys and girls do see each other at lunch. Often I've wished I could learn the simpler skills the girls ply, like producing rough fabrics on machines the men construct, but the one occasion on which I expressed such a desire to my father is one I'm not likely to forget. I was younger then and hadn't learned better.

"I wasn't there," I say tiredly.

"I know," she says, a look of eager horror on her face. "You were outside. Helena saw you go this morning. So what was it like?"

My eyes are already straying down the corridor toward escape. How can I explain what it was like today? I'm too confused. "It's the Wrecker's workshop out there, truly," I say, pulling away. "Look, I'm sorry, but I need to get home."

She lays a cool hand on my arm. She's very pretty with her enviably long yellow hair, and she's nearly as tall as I am. "Jude, what's wrong?" she asks, her face close to mine, eyes filled with concern. "Was it that horrible? You can tell me."

I want to weep. I have friends, sure, or I did, but what I've never had is someone I can confide in, someone I can really trust and open up to. That's all I want.

"Sariah—"

I feel her eyes searching my face, but I can't quite meet her gaze. "What is it?" she says.

"I—" Am I really going to say it? She's always been nice to me, kind. I glance up quickly. "What do you think about Nic?"

"Nicodemus?" A little crease appears between Sariah's fine eyebrows. "He's okay, he's nice. Why?"

I shake my head, my stomach turning inside out. "It's just—you know, he's such a great guy…"

I trail off as her eyes get a little wider. "Oh," she says

quietly, almost in wonder.

"I mean, he's been my best friend for such an incredibly long time," I say.

She nods slowly, focused on some inner vision. "No, no, I see. I get it."

"So, you know . . ."

"Who would have thought?" The ghost of a pensive smile touches the corner of her mouth. She kisses me suddenly on the cheek. "Thank you, Jude. Thank you. I'll talk to you later."

With that she trails off down the corridor, yellow hair billowing in the quarter-g, leaving me to wonder desolately what in space just happened.

THOMAS IS WAITING FOR ME AT THE CABIN, READ-ing the Manual. He looks pointedly at his chronometer as the hatch closes behind me. "I expected you sooner," he says.

"I stopped for devotions on the way back," I say. "I thought I might be too tired later."

He nods, accepting this, and I breathe a sigh of relief. "How was it today?" he asks.

I shrug. "Fine, I guess."

"Did you work hard?"

"I think I did."

"Crew treat you okay?"

I take off my cap and rub my head. I don't want to get into it all with Thomas. "They were fine. They didn't pay me much mind."

Thomas closes his Manual, a finger marking his place. "You be polite around them, Jude, but keep your thoughts to yourself. That's the way to stay true among the Sculpted."

"I will," I say, though already I feel duplicitous.

Thankfully, that seems to close that subject. The only other thing Thomas seems to want to know before he goes back to his reading is when I expect to be paid— something I haven't given much of a thought to. I assumed that was something he would have worked out with Renny already.

I prepare our dinner on the foldout stovetop, a stew of ground meat, beans, and vegetables. The activity proves more calming and centering to me than devotions did. But that night as I drift toward sleep, my mind keeps turning back to the women in the locker room, and to the wooden chest bolted to the deck not two feet from my head. Kaiya's chest.

THE SCREW IS A PECULIAR MACHINE, PARTAKING directly as it does of aspects of the Axle, the Inclined Plane, and the Wedge, and often requiring application of the Lever to fulfill its purpose. This is fitting, given its function as the aspect that both joins together and elevates, and as a representation of the way in which men and women join together in holy communion with the Builder to ignite the spark of life.

Sacred as it is, I've always been a little embarrassed by the Screw, a little wary of it. Maybe if that were my ward I'd have a better understanding of it, a healthier attitude toward it, but I've never been quite comfortable with its symbolic freight. Love and apotheosis strike me as less the Screw's nature than doing violence to whatever surface it encounters.

I find it difficult to credit that I will ever come to completely trust and adore the Screw.

My work schedule is seven days on and three off—one full s-week as reckoned by the Sculpted. My first "weekend" falls on a Thursday through Saturday by the Guild calendar, which means schola every day while I'm supposed to be taking a break. Neither my long stretches without a day of rest nor my falling behind at schola seems to bother Thomas much, but it bothers me. When I dare bring this up, he tells me the Builder is blessing us for our sacrifice—though I don't see what sacrifice it is that he's making.

By my second s-week on the job, I've begun to feel comfortable and confident in null-g, and competent if not so comfortable with my fishbowl's graphic overlay. It's as if I'm looking at a raw and exposed layer of reality that should more properly be covered, or at the very least from which I should avert my eyes—though, just as in the locker room with my crewmates, doing so is practically not an option. I am on friendly terms with most of the crew, even if I can't quite bring myself to consider any of them friends. We're too different for that, both in our worldviews and in our expectations of what friendship means. For one thing, they don't seem to have a problem with the occasional tweaking of one another's anatomy in the showers. I do, as they have learned.

I have spent most of my lunch hours and several more walks home chatting with Derek. Despite the fact that he's so obviously unlike me, he has a directness, a curiosity, and a willingness to take my arguments seriously that I can't help but like, even if I can't always effectively rebut the points he makes. I consider him a goad to make me apply myself more diligently to my studies. I retain the faith that answers exist to his objections, and if I can't find them and express them articulately then I'm hardly a worthy ambassador for the Guild.

It's end of shift on Sevenday of my second s-week on the job when Renny calls us together in the break room. "Got some news, little stevies," she says, executing a sort of four-handed cartwheel up a chair to perch on her favorite table. The animated chatter anticipating our weekend break quiets down.

"Fourday and Fiveday next week we've got a special assignment coming up for anyone who wants in on it. Berth A-11, prospecting ship full of scientific samples. Very delicate, both the ship and the cargo. Berth's gonna be fully evacuated, so there's hazard pay, but only those of you rated for vacuum will be eligible. If you don't want in, that's fine—we'll have plenty to do here. But if you want in and you're not vacuum-rated, it's not too late to get that way. You can even take shift time to do it without getting docked. I just need to see your certification first thing Threeday if you want in. Understood? All right, that's it."

Renny draws me aside as the others file off to the showers. "This is a good opportunity, kid," she tells me in a low voice. "You're a good worker, and you sure don't want to miss out on triple pay."

She's right, I don't. I can imagine how happy Thomas will be to see the extra credits. "How do I get vacuum-rated?" I ask, watching two tiny, distorted me's in her silvery eyeglobes. "Is there a test I take or something?"

"Not, er, not really," Renny says. "What it mostly entails is getting your lungs and eyes and ears vacuum-hardened. You'd be wearing a pressure suit in the berth, of course, but if it should fail you could suffocate before we got you out of there and repressurized. Regs don't let us subject you to that risk."

My breath catches. "What you're talking about—that would mean Sculpting, wouldn't it?"

"Just a small bit, internally."

The pay would be welcome, but I have to shake my head. "No offense, but I can't do that. I'm very sorry."

Renny shrugs, an elaborate motion of her hind shoulders. My reflection dances crazily in her eyes. "What can I say, kid? It's your choice, and I sure won't think any worse of you for it. But don't make the decision now. Think about it over the break. Get the details from Geoff. Talk to your old man, see what he says."

"Right," I say. "I already know what he'd tell me."

"Thomas ain't a bad guy, for a Wheelie. Talk to him, kid."

All the way to the showers, cringing, I can hear Thomas telling me the Wrecker's in me. But I can't quite shake Renny's insistence that I bring it up with him.

THAT EVENING OVER OUR HUMBLE DINNER I blurt
it out before I can reconsider: "Renny says there's a special job next week. Extra pay, and she's pushing me to
do it."

Thomas puts down his fork. "And?" he says, glaring at
me over the table.

"And . . . I'd need some small modifications. Vacuum-hardening."

Thomas bows his head. Today's a Saturday in the
Quarter, what would in other circumstances have meant
half a day at schola for me and a morning of light com-
munity service for him. But neither of us follows a normal schedule now, and we're each exhausted from the
labors of the day. I wait for him to speak, not chewing,
heart in my throat.

Not that I don't know the right answer. I only have
to ask myself what the Builder would say. *Or my moth-*

er, I think, the tip of my nonslipper grazing the wooden chest beneath the foldout table that spans the width between the bunks. The chest contains Kaiya's clothing, which, despite the reg against storage of unnecessary mass, Thomas has never been able to bring himself to recycle. It's almost as if he's waiting for her to come back. I'm not, though. I don't have many firm memories of Kaiya, and in fact Thomas has told me so often that my mother is with the angels now that that's how I nearly always picture her: dressed in spotless white with huge feathered wings furled above her, looking down on me from on high. I know what she would think if I broached the topic of transfiguration. I know what she does think, in whatever level of the Builder's mansion she's watching me from.

At last Thomas forks a bite of boiled potatoes and carrots into his mouth and peers at me, practically through me, from under lowered brows. "You told her no, right?"

I flinch a little. It takes a moment for me to realize he's talking about Renny, not Kaiya. "Of course," I say. My words feel defensive, as if he's somehow already forced me to lie to him.

"Wrecker take that woman, anyway." He shovels more food into his mouth and chews silently for a few bites.

When he speaks again his voice and his eyes, unexpectedly, have softened. "Son, I know they teach us at temple never to compromise with the world, to always live as if we're with the Builder in his mansion, but in practice that's just impossible. We all make compromises—we have to, or we couldn't get by. We couldn't live.

The tricky part—no, the *hard* part is knowing what's okay to compromise and what isn't. You have to figure out where that dividing line is—and then stay well back from it. When you try to walk it…"

Thomas folds his hands together and stares down at the table. "Jude, son, I can tell you what happens. You fall. You tell yourself you won't, but you do." He clears his throat, lips compressing almost convulsively. "I just want you to be happy. Maybe that's not what this world is for, but Builder knows it's what I want for you."

His eyes rove this way and that, never meeting mine, and he clears his throat again. Once upon a time, this would have been where I edged around the table to give him an awkward hug. Tonight I can't. My soul cries for him, but I'm not a little kid anymore, and I just can't.

We finish our meal in silence.

THE NEXT DAY IS TEMPLE, THE FIRST SUNDAY IN three Guild weeks I've been off work. Thomas and I sit toward the back of the long, low chapel, which sits near the AD Gate at the opposite end of the Quarter from the PM Gate. The bulkheads are of brushed gray metal, with three of the Six Machines etched on the left wall, three on the right, and the carpenter's square on the wall behind the pulpit.

Inclined Plane Ward meets third every Sunday, in the late-morning slot. During Foreman Saul's sermon after the sacrament, I spot Nicodemus several rows ahead and to the right. What caught my eye was his golden head tilting back as he smiled wide at something the person next to him had whispered in his ear. The person next to him has long, shining yellow hair.

The person next to him is Sariah.

I blink hard for the next several minutes. I shift and

fidget through the rest of the sermon. The pew is cold and rigid—dumb, unyielding matter—and no matter how I try I can't get comfortable. I'm supposed to meet the foreman for my private instruction after church, but when the service ends I rush back to the cabin instead, with a vague excuse to Thomas about my stomach.

Two full days of schola still ahead, catching up on subjects where I'm falling further and further behind, before I get to return to work. I don't know how I'm going to make it.

WEDNESDAY COMES AT LAST, ONEDAY TO THE
rest of the station, and in the break room in the early
morning Renny reminds the gathered crew that we have
only two days left to sign up and show vacuum certification if we want in on the special gig. She looks my way
but I duck my eyes. Funny—I've spent the past two days
at schola avoiding Nic and looking forward to Oneday,
and now that it's here it looks like I'm going to spend the
day avoiding Renny. I'm such a bent nail I can't stand
myself.

Our client today is a Thunder-class starship, *Colder
Equation*, which we lade with supplies bound for the ex-
omorph colony at Van Maanen's Star. It's hard work but
mostly mindless, and I find my cares evaporating for the
first time in days. I feel best at midshift when we break
for lunch, but the rest of the day is marred by the clock
in the corner of my vision, ticking down the minutes un-

til I return to gravity's embrace.

At shift's end, after showers, I ask Derek if he'd like to go somewhere for food. He's invited me to eat after work several times now, but I've worried not just that Thomas would find out but that I wouldn't be able to find anything appetizing in the public cafeterias. Tonight, though, I'm desperate enough to talk that I think I can overcome my food objections.

Delighted, Derek leads me all the way to a dim cafeteria two levels in from the rim. I'm not sure what I was expecting, but certainly not this gloomy cave with the dark red walls and the low ceiling. Quiet, lilting string music plucked out by unseen hands drifts on the air, which smells gently dank and laden with minerals. Thick pillars and curtains of leafy plant life obscure the view from one end of the place to the other, though here and there I can see tables of two, three, or four, the sometimes asymmetrical faces of the patrons lit from below by flickering orange light. Perhaps it's the dimness, but I no longer find their deformities as hideous as I did at first.

A woman in a lumpy black cowled robe leads us through the compact maze of foliage to a table against a black-painted bulkhead studded with white pinpricks. It isn't until we take our seats in form-fitting smart-matter chairs that I realize the bulkhead isn't a bulkhead at all, but a viewport—a hole punched through fifteen centimeters of metal and plugged with glass or something like it.

"Wheel and Axle," I murmur, stunned. I can't take my

eyes from the bright, nail-hard stars.

"Netherheim and Freya should come into view before you're finished," the cowled woman says. "That's a sight to behold." She makes an arcane gesture in the air. "Now, let me call your attention to today's specials."

"Perhaps a . . . hardcopy menu would be in order for my friend here?" Derek says, nodding toward me.

"Oh, certainly," the woman says before receding like smoke into the shadows.

The surface of our table glows a dim, swirling orange, making Derek's skin look like polished stone and his eyes smolder with fire. "So what do you think?" he asks.

"It's not what I expected at all. I pictured something more, well, functional from a cafeteria."

"Cafeteria, eh?" Derek's eyes sparkle with amusement. "I suppose you could think of it that way."

The robed woman returns with a catalog of dishes listed on a single sheet of paper, and I'm shocked to discover, as Derek points out, that most of the items have been grown hydroponically. "This must be terribly expensive," I say, mouth watering. "I can't afford this, I'm sure of it."

"Relax," Derek says. "Everyone gets credit for a meal like this once a month. I've got a couple saved up, and you must have at least a dozen just sitting there, unused."

I cover my surprise and confusion by studying the menu. I have the sense of riding an iceberg in a limitless ocean, borne up by a vast bulk the composition of which I can't begin to fathom. Choosing more or less at random, I select an opener of fine pasta garnished with grated cheeses and truffle shavings, and a spiced squash tart as a main course. Derek places our orders, a process invisible to me, choosing a fruit assortment and a roulade of vegetables and nuts for himself.

He folds his hands and leans forward. "So, what's on your mind, Jude?"

"Oh, this and that," I say, and shrug. "I was thinking today about what it would be like to live out in space."

Derek shakes his head, grinning. "We do live in space. Or hadn't you noticed?"

"No, I mean *in* space, like the exomorphs, just floating there in the middle of nothing."

"Well, it's not nothing. There is a structure, a lattice, to grow their colony in."

"But it's not much, and it's open to space." I didn't know there were such creatures, such people, until today. I read it on the fishbowl during work. "Can you even imagine the mods you'd need for that?"

"Serious work indeed," Derek says. "Not to be undertaken lightly."

"No one on our crew has work that serious. They all look pretty much normal, at least when they're dressed."

"The more radical mods are often specialization for particular types of work. We're unskilled labor, our crew, Jude."

I nod, having figured this out without really being able to articulate it. I take a deep breath. "Derek, can I ask you something personal?"

He laces his fingers together and rests his joined hands on the table. The green of his palms has crept halfway up his arms in the time since I met him, and his ears are now tinged green as well, though I can't make the hues out well in this light. His gaze upon me is very open and direct and unsettling, more so because every day I come to know better how little I understand of his world, layered as it is above and beneath and around mine. "I don't know, can you?" he says.

"I don't know. I'll try." I've learned some things about him from the fishbowl at work without really trying—for instance, the distressing fact that he has three biological mothers—but nothing that doesn't just whet my curiosity. I look down at the glowing table and take a deep breath. "I'm just wondering if there's some, I don't know, some practical reason for your mods, something functional. You know, what the blue skin turning green is all about."

"There's a time for love, and a time to hate," Derek says with a rakish smile. "A time for blue, and a time for green."

I puff out an exasperated breath. "Do you spend all your time looking up things in the Manual you can make fun of?"

He shakes his head. "You do understand, don't you, Jude," he says animatedly, "that a book called the Bible existed long before Titus Grant slapped his own generic title on it, and that it's not exactly an obscure work in the human literary canon?"

"High Foreman Titus didn't just change the title. Under the Builder's inspiration, he clarified and corrected—"

Derek extends a finger until it almost touches my lips, waving his other hand preemptively. "Yes, fine. But you understand he didn't write the Manual from scratch."

"All right, fine, I understand," I say. "So what about the color change?"

He leans back in his chair. "Right, that. It's not really anything practical. There's nothing I can point to and say my skin color accomplishes. In fact, it's mostly a random aesthetic process. I'm never sure what color's coming up next."

"Then why did you do it? I mean, what's the purpose?"

"It keeps me interested," Derek says, and his smile cracks momentarily. "I see me and not-me in the mirror at the same time, and there's always the mystery of what's coming next. It's as good a reason to stick around as any." He leans forward again, and to my ears his heartiness now sounds forced. "What makes you curious, friend?"

I shake my head. "I don't know. Nothing."

"You're thinking about the job, aren't you? The vacuum job this Fourday."

I look out the viewport at the stars, but the view seems to tilt and wheel beneath me, spinning my sense of balance away. "Maybe," I admit.

"You know," Derek says with a trace of his vigorous smile, "if you do it, a lot of folks on the crew are going to be disappointed. People are starting to get protective of you, and you may make them feel like they've corrupted you."

"It's not their decision," I say.

"Agreed."

A different woman brings us our opening course. A thick tail moving in counterpoint to the balanced trays in her hands protrudes from beneath her black robe. Attention to the food spares Derek and me from the burden of conversation. I'm not sure I enjoy all the lush, strange flavors on my plate, but I know I've never tasted anything so vivid. I swallow every last crumb.

Derek seems uncharacteristically fidgety between courses, but it's not until our main courses have arrived and I'm halfway through my tart—excellent—that he says, "Jude, can I ask you something?"

"Um, sure," I say between bites.

He swallows. "What is it that happened to your mother?"

The bite I've just taken feels too big going down my throat. "How do you know about my mother?"

"I'm sorry, I'm not trying to pry." He wipes his mouth with a cloth serviette that actually shows slight stains of use. "It's hard sometimes to look at you and not make the easy jumps back through your genealogy."

"My mother died when I was small, four or five," I say, setting down my fork and holding my gaze steady with great effort. "I'm not clear exactly how. My father doesn't like to talk about it, and I don't like to press him."

Derek opens his mouth, looking confused, and for a moment I have the strangest feeling he's going to tell *me* how it happened. I feel the sting beginning behind my eyes at the thought that he might know more about it than I do.

But what he says is: "Do you think about her much?"

I nod. "All the time."

He looks so stricken at this that I feel I could be looking at a reflection of my own expression in a blue-tinted mirror—or, so I believe for a giddy, wildly hopeful moment, at my mother. The illusion shatters as Derek rises suddenly in his chair, takes my face in both his green hands, and leans in to kiss me on the mouth. He stares at me a second or two, an eternity, and sits back down.

Breathless, I turn to the window. Netherheim has swung into view, a giant ball of spun sugar swirled with red and yellow stripes, a fruit as sweet and bursting and sick-making as my heart inside me. I sit very still, not looking at him. My pulse is racing about a hundred klicks a second.

"I don't know if I can finish this," I say and push the rest of my tart away.

"Jude, I'm sorry," Derek says, his eyes very steady and direct.

"Why did you do that?" I ask. Asking a question is better than yelling or crying or hitting the table.

Derek spreads his green palms. They look black with blood in the cafeteria's hellish light. "I forgot for a minute what a kiss signifies to your people. Let myself forget, to be honest. To us—the groups I identify with, at least—it can be a greeting between friends, a show of camaraderie or comfort, even the equivalent of a slap. It doesn't have to have a sexual connotation."

"But why did you do it?"

Derek sighs. "Jude, you just seemed so sad. I couldn't stand it. Lonely and sad." He shakes his head. "You reminded me of me when I was your age. Sometimes I wish someone had just done that for me."

Do I believe him? I'm not sure. I look out the viewport. Netherheim is just beginning to slide out of view. A cauldron of emotion, like the multicolored atmosphere of the planet below, seethes inside me. I want to storm out of the room. I want to turn a somersault in the air. I want to shake Derek by the shoulders until his head flops like a scrap doll's.

I think about Nicodemus, wondering what I ever saw in him.

"I'm sorry," I say. "Can you help me find an elevator to Level Six?"

"Of course, Jude."

The compassion and concern in Derek's voice are unbearable. So is the heartbreak.

At home, safe from the sea of wild bodies and leering faces that populate the station, I fall to my knees. I should pray to the Builder for forgiveness, for putting myself in such a compromised position, but instead I thumb the combination on the wooden chest in the middle of the deck. Thomas is still out, and with luck will be for at least another hour. He doesn't know that I long ago surfed the combination over his shoulder. The lid swings back on stiff, creaky, decidedly low-tech hinges, revealing the layered treasures within.

Reverently, I lift out the first folded garment, hearing in my mind a surreal ghost of Kaiya's voice telling Thomas to keep this, she'll have no use for it where she's going. I unfold and smooth out the soft gray dress with the Inclined Plane on the bosom—then, hands trembling, pull it over my head and slip my arms through the sleeves, as I've done maybe half a dozen times before in my life.

The fabric is tight across my shoulders and under my arms—much tighter than it was the time before. There's no hope of closing the buttons at the back. This may be the last time I can manage to fit into it at all.

Sobs rise up inside me as I yearn for angel wings to bear me away.

THE SENSATION OF WALKING SPINWARD INSIDE A great turning wheel like Netherview Station is a little like walking up an endless inclined plane. Because your feet are borne forward by the rotation a tiny bit faster than your head, you might feel if you're attentive enough as if you're leaning slightly backward, or walking up the slightest of slopes.

By the same token, a counterspinward stroll might feel a bit like a walk downhill. But compare your slight forward angle to a tangent of the circle your feet are touching and you'll see that the attitude of your body is more like that of a person walking uphill. Thus, walk either direction inside the rim of a rolling wheel and you partake of one aspect or another of ascending an incline.

I haven't found much scriptural support for my position, and the members of Wheel and Axle in particular would call it blasphemy, but at some crossroads it strikes me that any path you follow can lead you upward, and closer to the Builder.

I SLEEP BADLY, UNACCUSTOMED TO THE RICHNESS
of the food in my belly. Upon rising I prepare Thomas
what seems a meager and bland breakfast, all the while
fearing that he will somehow sense that the chest and
its contents have been disturbed. But he eats with all his
attention on his Manual, and he barely bats an eye when
I tell him I may end up working overtime today.

I arrive early at the hub, in time to catch Renny in her
spherical office well before the start of our Twoday shift.
"I want to learn more about this vacuum-hardening procedure," I tell her without preamble. "Uh, how can I do that?"

Renny vaults out of her chair like a charged parti-
cle expelled from an atom. "If you weren't crippled you
could ask from anywhere," she says, clinging to the
frame of the hatch and shoving her ugly face into mine.
"As it is, you'll have to use a Geoffroom. There's one not
far from here."

She leads me on a brisk walk. "You know," I say as I hurry to keep up with her, "my father's pretty upset with you."

Renny looks over her shoulder and grins. "What, for telling you about the job? Oh, I heard from him. Nothing he could do about it, though. It's regs and Thomas knows it. Like he has room to complain, the way he called in so many favors to get a barefooter like you onto the team in the first place. But he's your father and he's just following the script, same as me."

She stops before a row of three hatches, each emblazoned with the old-fashioned schematic symbol for an activated light fixture. I've passed hatches like these at many times since starting my job, but never known what they were.

Renny rears up on her hind arms and pats the gleaming surface of the first hatch. "Now here's the next part of my script," she says. "This is a Geoffroom, where Geoff can tell you anything you care to ask about. He'll answer all your questions and then some. The light bulb is glowing, which means the room's unoccupied and you can walk right in. Take all the time you need, but if you're going to be here longer than the first hour of shift, have the big lug message me so I know."

She touches a panel in the center of the hatch, and it opens with a slight hiss.

"Keep your eyes and ears open, kid," she says, and I step inside.

"**Don't be afraid. I won't bite.**"

The voice is a warm tenor and originates from no location I can see in this small, very white room. The ceiling is high enough to let me stand comfortably; my outstretched arms would nearly span the room in both dimensions. A body-enfolding chair like you might find at the medic's rests at the center of the deck. Panicked, I turn—to find the hatch has sealed noiselessly behind me. I can barely see its outline.

"Have a seat, Jude," the voice says. "We've got a lot to talk about."

The air is warm, but my skin prickles cold and hard. "Where are you?" I say. "How do you know my name?"

"I've known you since you were born, Jude. I'm glad we're finally getting a chance to talk. This happens so rarely with members of your Guild. But we'll talk more comfortably if you sit. Please."

Blasphemy! my mind cries. *False gods!* But I ease myself down into the chair, letting the cushions take hold of me. I feel the chair adjust to my size, and carefully I lay my head back in the niche that fits it.

A man appears before me. A pot-bellied man with flowing white hair and a bushy white mustache, dressed in a billowy white coverall. A man carrying a wooden carpenter's square. "Selah," he says.

I start in alarm, but the man makes calming motions as he bends over me. "The Builder," I gasp.

He shakes his head. "If you see me in the likeness of the Builder, it's only because that's your strongest conception of a figure of benevolent wisdom. Not to aggrandize myself at all." He looks down at the carpenter's square in his hand. "This probably doesn't help matters." He tosses the square over his shoulder, and it vanishes.

"Who are you?" I say, struggling to sit up.

The man crackles and flashes transparent. "This'll be less disorienting if you stay down in the chair," he says. "For both of us."

Suspiciously I lie back, and the image solidifies. In fact, I can feel the man as he presses a comforting hand to my chest and pushes me down.

"I'm Geoff," he says. "No last name, but I can give you a version number if you're really interested."

He smells faintly of sweat, smoke, and some kind of musky perfume. "I don't know what you mean," I say.

"I know," he says with a smirk. He pulls up a chair from nowhere, seats himself near my knees, and crosses his legs. "But you came here because you wanted to ask me something. So go ahead. Ask me anything you like. Ask me as much as you like. That's what I'm here for."

"What are you?" I ask.

"A very sophisticated information retrieval system. Once upon a time, you might have called me a search engine, but I'm much more than that. I'm something of a diagnostician as well, and a physician, and a surgeon, and a teacher and a tutor. A diplomat, a translator, an ombudsman. A legal advisor, and an advocate too. And I play a mean hand of gin."

"Where did you get the name Geoff?" I'm thinking of Derek and his name change. "What does it mean?"

Geoff strokes his mustache. "Nothing, really. I just liked the sound of it. It seemed to me to suit me somehow. Where did you get your name?"

I blink. "From the Manual."

"Be glad you didn't end up Nebuchadnezzar."

Maybe this is where Derek learned to be so cheeky. "How is it I can see you? It has something to do with the chair, doesn't it?"

"It has plenty to do with the chair, and with its ability to create a microwave interface with your visual cortex. I can give you a more detailed technical specification if you like, but I imagine you have more pressing questions you'd like to ask."

I'm delighted in spite of myself, and I raise my head out of the cradle several times in succession just to watch Geoff flicker in and out of existence.

"Careful," he says, rising from his illusory chair. "You'll make yourself sick."

He's right. My head has started pounding and the room whirls. My stomach feels none too steadfast in its grip on breakfast. I lie back and Geoff strokes my forehead. His cool fingers fail to disturb the swelling droplets of perspiration. I take deep breaths, digging my fingers into the padding of the armrests.

"Tell me about this vacuum-hardening process my boss keeps telling me about," I say, eyes squeezed shut. "How does it work?"

"There's not a lot to it," Geoff says in a reassuring tone. "What it does is construct around your lungs a sort of a cellular retaining wall that gets deployed on any catastrophic drop in air pressure. It actually seals shut your lungs and can temporarily prevent the gases in your bloodstream from expanding and killing you. This retaining wall is also capable of breaking oxygen atoms loose from the carbon dioxide your blood returns to your lungs, so you can effectively keep rebreathing the same old air. That's only temporary too, of course. It's like any filter—eventually it's going to get choked with carbon and fail. But you can last an hour that way, anyway. More than enough time for help to get to you. In most circumstances."

It sounds so reasonable when Geoff says it. I'm looking at him again now, and he has returned to his seat. "Is the procedure expensive?" I ask, praying the answer will be yes.

"Not at all," Geoff says. "And if you can demonstrate a need for it in the course of your job, the station covers it anyway. You do qualify, by the way."

"Are there side effects?"

"You might feel a little short of breath after the procedure, a little dizzy and weak, but your lungs will adjust within a day or so. That's all, really."

I take a deep breath. "And the procedure itself—it sounds complicated. How long does it take?"

"Oh, about twenty minutes," Geoff says, tilting his head to one side.

"Twenty minutes! That's all?"

"You'd have the entire shift off, though, for recovery and observation. With pay."

"But—but how is that possible?" I'm groping for words. "I mean, it's Sculpting, right? You can't just snap your fingers and it's done."

"That would be true, Jude . . . if we were starting from scratch. We're not."

Now I can't breathe, and my insides seem to freeze. "What do you—what do you mean?"

Geoff stands up and clasps his hands behind his back. "You *are* what you call Sculpted, Jude, as is every other member of the Machinist Guild on Netherview Station. You've been that way since before birth, the nanodocs passed on to you via your mother's bloodstream. Your nanodocs don't do anything more than maintain reasonably good health and let me keep tabs on you. But the potential is there for more. Much more."

"But—but why?" Tears gather in the corners of my eyes. "How can you do this to us? It's—it's monstrous!"

Geoff looks pained. "Jude, please understand what a fragile environment this station is. We have two million permanent residents and millions more who pass through every month. We can't have people running loose who aren't monitored in some way."

"But it's wrong. It's my body!"

"Jude, if I weren't helping out, your body would have broken the first time you left the Quarter. Your devotions keep your muscles strong, but the low gravity weakens your bones. You've had supplements in your food all your life to counteract the effects."

I roll my head from side to side. "Lies."

"I'm not lying, Jude."

"Not now, but all along! Everything we know, my people, it's all lies."

"I told you the first opportunity I had. Jude, you have the right to get this information at the age of ten, when you become a provisional citizen of Netherview Station—that's about thirteen and a third by your Guild calendar. Unfortunately, the Guild can keep that knowledge from you until age fifteen—twenty to you. You still have the right to ask and get answers, like you're doing now, but what good does that do most of you when you don't *know* you can ask?"

I'm shaking my head. "I don't believe you. That would mean—that would mean everyone knows. All the adults—my father. Everyone knows."

"Actually, no." Geoff purses his lips sadly and lays a hand on my arm. "Just because they know they have the right to ask doesn't mean they'll actually do it. By the time they reach twenty, most of them don't want to know."

"I don't want to know!" I say, wrenching my arm

through Geoff's hand to paw the water from my eyes. "Why are you telling me this?"

"Jude…"

"No! You're the Wrecker! I don't want to hear it."

Geoff sighs. "As far as I'm aware, I am not the Wrecker. In fact, I'm not certain I'm capable of telling a lie. I try my very best to do good, really."

Uncomfortably aware of how childish I'm being, I cross my arms and turn my head away from the preening phantom before me. I lie that way for some time, mind churning. When I look at Geoff again he's watching me expectantly. I feel hollow inside.

"Geoff," I say, my voice small, "can you fix my brain?"

Geoff leans forward, looking concerned. "What's wrong with your brain, Jude?"

"I—I mean—"

"Yes?"

"I think I'm out of true." I'm almost whispering. "Bent."

"How do you mean?"

"You know."

"Pretend I don't."

I lick my lips. "I think I like boys." The admission leaves me feeling curiously flat, detached. "Can you fix me?"

Geoff tugs at his white mustache. "Jude, there are various therapy regimens I can initiate, but I don't 'fix' things like sexual inclination. Not that I'd call you homosexual at all in the sense you'd think of it. The truth, I believe, is rather more interesting and complicated than that."

My heart leaps. "What's the truth?"

"Your Guild likes to treat sexuality and gender as binary values, either this or that, one right, one wrong, no other possibilities. But the ones you call Sculpted understand these characteristics more as a spectrum of possible values, fluid and multidimensional. There's no either-or, nor even necessarily a permanent identification with any given point on the grid." Geoff spreads his hands in an eerily Builderlike gesture. "Now, this is a preliminary diagnosis only, but you would appear to me to suffer from a multivalent somatocognitive dysphoria."

"A what?" I ask, vague trepidation gnawing at my stomach.

"To put it more bluntly, your body is male, but the personality inside may be closer to the female end of the continuum. Not all the way there, of course, but more so than not."

I shake my head despite the nausea I feel. "No, no. That's ridiculous."

"You would have learned very early to hide the symptoms—the wants and behaviors your people wouldn't find acceptable in a little boy. But that, plus overcompensation in areas of archaically male pursuit, still wouldn't make them go away."

"You're crazy." The notion is offensive, repulsive. "The Builder doesn't make mistakes like that."

"In a perfect world, maybe not," Geoff says. "But this world's anything but perfect, and we all have to come to our own accommodations with that fact. Now, I can recommend and even direct a course of therapeutic

counseling, just as a starting point, and of course participation would be entirely up to—"

"No!" I shout. "Stop it!"

"Jude, let's at least talk about this for a—"

"You lying, false machine, shut up! I can't think."

Geoff folds his hands in his lap as I turn my eyes to
the white ceiling, chewing the inside of my cheek. I'm
furious, and terrified for my soul, to realize how easily
I've been taken in by the lies of this Wrecker-spawned
abomination. The right thing to do—the right degree of
compromise—has never been more clear.

"I'm going to do it," I say, the steel in my voice a wall
holding back utter dissolution.

"I'm sorry—do what?" Geoff asks.

"The vacuum-hardening. I'm going to do it."

"Are you sure?" He sounds dubious.

"Absolutely. But so you don't get any ideas, I'm doing
it for the Guild, not for myself."

"I'm not certain what you mean by that."

"The more hazard pay I get," I say, "the more quickly
my people can get off this godforsaken station."

"Your pay is yours. It doesn't have to go to your Guild."

"I don't care."

"It won't make any difference," Geoff says. "The
Guild's debts are considerable."

"I don't care."

"Jude, I don't want you doing this under any false il-
lusions. The Guild owes so much money they can't even
pay the interest on it. It's practically a losing proposition
to keep housing them."

"Then why don't you just let them leave?" I demand, enraged.

Geoff shakes his head. "I'll tell you if you really want to know—that's my function. But you won't like it."

"I don't like it already! Just tell me."

"As you wish. I have to be concerned about the well-being of the station as a whole, and having you here serves a purpose other than economic. The existence of a permanent underprivileged social class reinforces in the minds of the rest of the population the benefits of full participation in this pseudo-socialist post-scarcity paradise of ours. Superiority breeds contentment, of a sort."

"So you're telling me my people live in poverty to provide an example of how undesirable poverty is?"

"I told you you weren't going to like it."

My anger has shrunk to a cold, clear gem in my heart. "As if it took a supercomputer to figure that out. And I told you I'd made up my mind already."

"Well!" he says, raising his eyebrows. He looks as if he's about to offer more argument, but evidently decides otherwise. "So you give your consent for the vacuum-hardening procedure?"

I give a curt nod. "Yes."

"So be it," Geoff says quietly. He almost sounds chastened. "I'll let your boss know you'll be occupied today, and we'll get started right away."

I arrange myself stiffly in the chair, arms at my sides, as if waiting for the lid of my coffin to close.

"You're all right from here?" Derek asks.

We're standing at the PM Gate, the smells and tumult and humidity around us as heavy as ever. His arm around my shoulder helps offset the crushing gravity. I nod a little woozily and say, "It'll be easier inside. Quarter gee."

As the end of the procedure drew near, Geoff roused me to suggest I might want a friend to walk me home. I said Derek's name before I really thought it through, but even after the fact, wondering if that had been a good idea, it didn't seem to me I really had a better option. Geoff contacted him, and Derek was there waiting outside the Geoffroom as soon as the hatch opened.

Now he takes his arm from around me and watches with concern as I take a wobbly step on my own. "Is this … you know … are you going to be in trouble?"

"How will anyone know?" I say. "There's nothing visible that's changed."

Derek looks like he's about to say something, then extends his hand instead. Green is now his predominant hue; even his irises have changed color. "Well, Jude, just in case . . . you've got a place to bunk down if you need it. No strings, just a place to stow your gear."

I nod, my throat thickening. I try to say thank you, but I can't. I duck my eyes, pull the lever, and pass through the gate.

I might be imagining it, but as the gate closes behind me I almost think I hear Derek saying, "Selah, Jude."

Inside, it's late and the corridors are empty. This is good because even in the lower grav I'm having trouble walking a straight line. Geoff told me this is nothing to worry about, that I'll feel fine again by morning, but drawing the wrong kind of attention on the way home through the Quarter *would* be something to worry about.

The cabin is dark when I slip inside, and Thomas lies motionless in his bunk. I strip off my coverall as quietly and cautiously as possible, crank down my bunk, and slip beneath the blanket. I lie on my back, unable to relax or even close my eyes. I spent most of the day in essentially this position. Like Geoff promised, the process took only twenty minutes—though, having felt nothing, I have only his word for that—but for the rest of my shift and beyond I lay fitfully dozing as I recuperated. I suspect Geoff would have liked to keep me longer than he did, but my father would have been livid if didn't come home all night.

My heart pounds as I suddenly become aware that Thomas is sitting up. I try to fake deep, easy breathing as

Thomas stands and pads across the narrow cabin. Even talking to him right now is too exhausting a thought to contemplate.

"Son," he says, almost a question, his voice subdued.

I crack an eye. His face is a gray smear in the darkness, gazing down on me like the cinders of a burnt-out sun.

"Son ... Jude ..." He sighs, breath hitching like an unbalanced motor. "I've been thinking a lot. Praying hard. I think it was wrong to send you to work. You can quit if you like. We'll get by. We'll manage."

I'm not sure he knows I'm awake, sees my eyes wide and dilated in the dark. It's like he's talking to himself. But when he reaches down to stroke my hair, his face draws nearer and his brows knit.

"Son?" he says, his voice quavering. "Son, what have they ... what have *you* ...?"

His hand snaps back like the magnetic arm of a relay switch. But I have only an instant to steel myself before he shakes off the stun and whips back, seizing me by my throat and one thigh and hauling me off the bunk.

"What in the Wheel have you done?" he cries, stumbling back as I watch the indistinct room tumble crazily around me. He loses his grip on my thigh, and my knees bounce off the deck even as my windpipe grinds against his other hand. I smash sideways against the bottom of the hatch, torn loose now from both his hands, and watch in the terrible clarity of low gravity as his leg swings back in an arc that will ultimately reverse and connect with my ribs.

I've never felt revulsion before at his correctional touch, only the sort of accepting resignation born of an intimate belief in the justice of it. But now, sprawled on the deck, my skin crawls with a sense of wrongness and violation.

Spasming, I curl myself around his leg at the moment of contact, I grab tight with both arms, I twist violently toward the hatch. Arms wheeling, Thomas hits the bulkhead face first.

The lights brighten at his startled cry, and in the sudden glare I scuttle desperately to the cabin's far corner. Thomas's face leaves a lurid red smear on the door as he slides to the deck. Dizzy, I push myself to my feet, lungs heaving, alternately holding back sobs and retches.

Thomas huddles on the floor with his arms over his head. "Oh, Builder," he half coughs, half wails. "What did you do?"

There's only one way he could have detected my mods. "You see it," I say, nodding like a drunk. "You're Sculpted too, you hypocrite."

He rolls over onto one side. "I couldn't do my job otherwise," he says, wiping blood from his mouth. "The job I have to do for you and our people. You have no idea what I've sacrificed."

"If I have no idea," I shout, "it's because you never told me! You sent me out there to face the same choices, but you never told me what *you* chose!"

He sits up, wiping his face and examining the blood on his hand. "I told you what was right, Jude. That's my job."

"You think I can't figure that out for myself?"

"Obviously not. Just like your mother." He's breathing hard, wincing. "She couldn't make the distinction either—what one person sacrifices out of necessity, and what that spares the rest of his family. She tore us apart because of it. She left this family in shambles." He pushes himself to his feet. "And I suppose you want to join her now, Wrecker take you both."

He totters the few steps toward me. I try to rise, intending to meet his assault on my feet, however it comes.

When he lays hands on me, though, it's to take my elbow and help me rise. "Be my guest," he says, gesturing to the hatch. "The door's there."

"The door?" I repeat, confused. "But . . . I thought . . ."

"Thought what? Thought—" Understanding dawns on his face like it hasn't yet on mine. "Oh, Jude."

"What?"

"You know so much else. I thought you must have found that out too."

I feel a tremble in my chest. "Found out what?"

"About your mother. That she's . . ."

Time seems to freeze. Something terrible roars somewhere far, far away, someplace only I can hear it.

"Son?" Something in my expression causes Thomas to release my elbow and take a step back. "Son," he says, hands up, "she *was* dead to us, dead in every way that mattered. She wasn't the same woman anymore. That woman died."

I fling myself at him, fists pummeling his chest like I'm a two-year-old throwing a tantrum.

"I was only trying to protect you, Jude! She's a monster now! She's Wreckerspawn!"

"Liar!" I cry, spittle flying from my mouth, tears blinding my eyes. "You liar!"

Now he's crying too, behind his upthrust arms, but it can't be from my pathetic beating. I shove him away in disgust. He staggers and sits down hard on his bunk. Not pausing to think, I snatch my clothing from the netted basket beside my bunk and cross to the hatch.

"And now you're leaving me, too," Thomas says bitterly. "You're her son in every way."

"Good," I say, turning the knob. "That's what I'd rather be anyway."

I have one last glimpse of him—hunched on his bunk in the harsh light like a wild animal, clawing at his wet, puffy eyes—and the hatch snicks shut behind me.

STANDING OVER ME, KAIYA LOOKS THE SAME AS she does in my half-waking imaginings—tall, porcelain-skinned with cascades of black hair, slightly larger than life, and no older than I remember. And those wings. Those glorious, glowing, white wings, stretching up into the inky night to touch at a point as far above her head as her head is above her feet. Each feather is as long and wide as one of my forearms. I could see her clasping me to her white-robed breast and soaring high out of the galactic plane with wings like that. She *is* an angel.

"Jude, first let me tell you how sorry I am," she says, leaning in so close I can count every one of her eyelashes. "I must have made a dozen recordings like this for you, at least, every time I move or make some other change, but sorry is the one thing that's always constant. That and how much I love you."

She's not here, of course, but I can almost smell the

dry perfume of her hair, the oily tang of her wings. I'm in a Geoffroom, the first one I could find, dressed and tipped back in the big chair and submerged in illusion. I can hardly believe this is happening, that this revelation has been so close to hand for so long, dormant and unguessed-at. All I had to do was ask the right question—or rather, to learn there were questions to ask at all. The magic incantation which had summoned this genie forth from the bottle was, quite simply, "Where is my mother?"

"I'm not authorized to answer that directly," Geoff told me. "But I do have a message for you."

"I wanted to bring you with me. Really I did, Jude. Not a day goes by that I don't wish I could. But because of the Guild's legal arrangements with the Station, that was impossible, and after the change I'd made I certainly couldn't stay. All I could do was hope that you reached a point—and preferably long before you reached your Guild majority—where you were able to start asking questions.

"Since you're seeing this, apparently you have.

"As I speak, you're now ten years old—thirteen by Guild reckoning. You're old enough to get this message if you ask, but not old enough that I can contact you directly. I don't know anything about you, what kind of young man you've turned into since the last time I saw you. Are you still as sweet as you were as a child, and as serious? What do you believe? What do you hope for? What do you dream? How have you changed? One thing's for certain—you must have changed some to be seeing this now. You must have made some hard choices, and you must have many more still to come.

"I'm still changing, too, Jude. I'm heading into the final phases of my exomorphological transform. When you see this, I'll probably already be homesteading in the New Bountiful Colony at Van Maanen's Star. It's a long way from here, terribly far. But that doesn't mean I won't drop it all to see you again. It won't be quick or simple, but if you want to start arranging it, just tell Geoff yes at the end of this recording, or any time afterward. A message will be dispatched to me immediately, though it may take a while to reach me.

"If you don't want to see me"—she shrugs, and her mighty wings tremble—"well, you can just say nothing. I'll never know, and I can go on assuming you've never seen this."

Is there really any question? Is there any doubt? "Yes, Mom," I say, feeling my face crumple. "Yes, yes, yes, yes, yes!"

"I'm so proud of you, Jude," she says. "You chose enlightenment over ignorance, and that's a terribly hard choice to make. I love you and I always will, no matter what. I can't wait for you to see what I've become, and I especially can't wait to see what you've become."

THE MANUAL TELLS US THAT IN THE BEGINNING the Builder decreed six fundamental machines. These are his six aspects, and all we do we must do with the Six. We need no other machines.

I believe this with all my heart. But not even my sincerest belief, I fear, is sufficient to make it true. Not when the shape of the Builder's seventh great Machine, transcending the other six, is coming clear.

The Seventh Machine is me.

About the Author

William Shunn's more than thirty works of short fiction have appeared everywhere from *Asimov's Science Fiction Magazine* to *Salon*, garnering nominations for the Hugo, Nebula, and Theodore Sturgeon Memorial Awards. His memoir, *The Accidental Terrorist: Confessions of a Reluctant Missionary*, was shortlisted for the Association for Mormon Letters Award. An off-and-on resident of New York City, he currently lives and writes in Harlem.

Learn more at shunn.net or at shunn.substack.com.

Printed in the USA
CPSIA information can be obtained
at www.ICGtesting.com
CBHW020830201124
17447CB00009B/74